THIS CANDLEWICK BOOK BELONGS TO:

_____

_____

_____

_____

sleeping

dancing

crying

waving

giving

eating

skipping

telling

listening

thinking

yawning

kicking

smelling

stroking

giving

shouting

washing

writing

singing

tearing

For Mark

Copyright © 1993 by Shirley Hughes

First U.S. paperback edition 1995

Library of Congress Cataloging-in-Publication Data

Hughes, Shirley.
Giving / Shirley Hughes.—1st U.S. ed.
Summary: A little girl and her baby brother experience the
various aspects of giving, finding that it is nice whether you are
giving a present, a smile, or a kiss.
ISBN 1-56402-129-7 (hardcover)—ISBN 1-56402-556-X (paperback)
[1. Generosity—Fiction.   2. Gifts—Fiction.]   I. Title.
PZ7.H87395Gi   1993   92-53002
[E]—dc20

2 4 6 8 10 9 7 5 3 1

Printed in Hong Kong

The pictures in this book were done in colored pencil,
watercolor, and pen line.

Candlewick Press
2067 Massachusetts Avenue
Cambridge, Massachusetts 02140

Giving

Shirley Hughes

CANDLEWICK PRESS
CAMBRIDGE, MASSACHUSETTS

I gave Mom a present on her birthday,
all wrapped up in pretty paper.

And she gave me a big kiss.

I gave Dad a very special picture
that I painted at play group.

And he gave me a ride on his
shoulders most of the way home.

I gave the baby some
slices of my apple.

We ate them sitting under the table.

At dinnertime the baby gave me
two of his soggy bread crusts.

That wasn't much of a present!

You can give someone an angry look . . .

or a big smile!

You can give a tea party . . .

or a seat on a crowded bus.

On my birthday Grandma and Grandpa
gave me a beautiful doll carriage.
I said "Thank you," and gave
them each a big hug.

And I gave my dear Bemily
a ride in it, all the way down the
garden path and back again.

I tried to give the
cat a ride too,

but she gave me a
nasty scratch!

So Dad had to give my poor arm
a kiss and a Band-Aid.

Sometimes, just when
I've built a big castle
out of blocks,

the baby comes along and
gives it a big swipe!
And it all falls down.

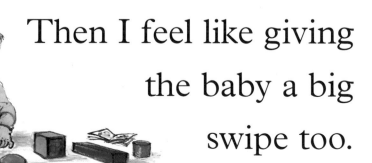

Then I feel like giving
the baby a big
swipe too.

But I don't, because

he *is* my baby brother, after all.

sleeping

dancing

crying

waving

giving

eating

skipping

telling

listening

thinking

yawning

kicking

smelling

stroking

giving

shouting

washing

writing

singing

tearing

SHIRLEY HUGHES's affectionate drawings, unique warmth, and deep understanding of family life have given her a special place in the hearts of children and parents everywhere. Her many books, including *The Big Concrete Lorry* and *Out and About*, have received international acclaim. She says that "*Giving* is a very simple, accessible book intended for sheer enjoyment. But tucked inside is a small lesson about 'doing' words."

Also by Shirley Hughes:

Bouncing
Chatting
Hiding